To Mamaw & Papaw's House

beehive cookie jar

tractor cups

war medal

coal miner portrait

CRANBERRY 1955

painted saw blade

WEST VIRGINIA

Let Me Fix You a Plate

A Tale of Two Kitchens · Elizabeth Lilly

NEAL PORTER BOOKS

HOLIDAY HOUSE / NEW YORK

For Anayah, who wasn't there yet —E.L.

Neal Porter Books

Text and illustrations copyright © 2021 by Elizabeth Lilly

All Rights Reserved

HOLIDAY HOUSE is registered in the U.S. Patent and Trademark Office.

Printed and bound in April 2021 at C&C Offset, Shenzhen, China.

The artwork for this book was made using pen-and-ink, colored pencil, and illustration markers.

Book design by Jennifer Browne

www.holidayhouse.com

First Edition

10 9 8 7 6 5 4 3 2 1

Library of Congress Cataloging-in-Publication Data

Names: Lilly, Elizabeth (Elizabeth Marie), author, illustrator.

Title: Let me fix you a plate : a tale of two kitchens / Elizabeth Lilly.

Description: First edition. | New York : Holiday House, [2021] | Audience:
  Ages 4–8 | Audience: Grades K–1 | Summary: A girl describes her family's
  annual visit with Mamaw and Papaw in West Virginia, then Abuela and
  Abuelo in Florida, especially the foods and cultural elements that make
  each kitchen unique.

Identifiers: LCCN 2019022754 | ISBN 9780823443253 (hardcover)

Subjects: CYAC: Grandparents—Fiction. | Vacations—Fiction.
  Family life—West Virginia—Fiction. | Family life—Florida—Fiction.
  Hispanic Americans—Fiction. | West Virginia—Fiction.
  Florida—Fiction.

Classification: LCC PZ7.1.L547 Let 2021 | DDC [E]—dc23

LC record available at https://lccn.loc.gov/2019022754

ISBN 978-0-8234-4325-3 (hardcover)

Once a year, on a Friday night,
my family leaves the city
and drives for hours and hours . . .

. . . to a mountain in West Virginia.

My Mamaw opens the door into the cool, dark night.
"Let me fix you a plate," she says.

Mamaw's midnight kitchen is warm and light,

with blue tiles on the floor and cat plates on the wall.

Mamaw's morning kitchen is clean and bright, with sausage sizzling in the skillet, blackberry jam on toast, and tractors on cups.

My Papaw drinks his coffee with cream but no sugar,
and Daddy does too. My dad and his dad,
Daddy and Papaw, with the same coffee cups.

Outside the stray cat who lives
in the old trailer meows
and morning mountain fog
wrinkles and rolls.
Later my sisters stack
vanilla wafer cookies,

Mamaw pours the pudding,
and I cover the top
with slices of banana.
Then we eat it all.

Three days later
we leave Mamaw's house,
so early it is still night,

and drive and drive and drive,
south and south and south,
to a little orange house
on a patch of scratchy grass
in Florida.

We get out of the car and the hot, sticky air hugs us close.

Then Abuela runs out and hugs us even closer.
"Hay comidita adentro. Comense."
"There's food inside. Come and eat," she says.

In Abuela's midnight kitchen,
white tiles feel cool
under my feet.
Aunts and cousins
and uncles and neighbors
talk over each other
above my head.

I crunch tostones
and scoop arroz
and slurp flan and fall asleep
at the table,
my mom still laughing,
saying loud Spanish words
that I don't understand.

Outside Abuela's morning kitchen,

red ants climb over scratchy grass
and bite my feet while I pick naranjas
with Abuelo in the yard.

We drink them as juice and eat arepas
with queso blanco.

My mom helps her mom to fry the corn flour cakes.
My mom and her mom,
cooking and chatting together.

Abuelo teaches me Spanish words
while I look around.

"Boca" means mouth.

There are little wooden houses
from Puerto Rico, keys hanging below.

"Nariz" means nose.

A shelf of nothing but frog figurines,
glass and stone and wood.

"Oreja" means ear.

And a sliding glass door,
between air-conditioned room
and the sticky summer heat.

In the evening, Tio Elmer
makes coquito,
and the grown-ups drink the
coconut rum punch
that looks, but doesn't taste,
like eggnog.

I hide behind the couch with my book
while my cousins and aunts and uncles
dance salsa and merengue.

Abuela finds me
and gives me tostones.

Three days later we leave the little orange house
and drive and drive and drive
back toward our house in the city.

We stare at the changing scenery,
tummies full, hearts fuller,
already missing the

salsa
sausage
toast
tostones
ants
aunts
arepas
Abuela
naranjas
bananas
mountains
Mamaw
cats
and fog
and
scratchy grass.

We reach our house, tired and hungry.
I look at Mommy. She is tan and brown, bags under tired eyes,
missing Spanish words and oranges on trees.

I look at Daddy, pink from sunburn, messy hair and stubbled chin,
missing Mamaw's meals and quiet mountaintops.
"I'm hungry," I say.

So Mommy mixes flour,
and Daddy beats eggs.
I set syrup on the table.
Mommy's midnight kitchen
has bright lights
and warm wood floors,
plantain pressers
next to potato mashers.
Outside, our windows glow
like gems seen by
sleepy passing cars.
Inside there's warm, soft talk
and air that smells like waffles.
Daddy works the iron,
Mommy forks waffles onto plates,
and their three little pollitos,
hungry little chicks,
gobble them up . . .

. . . and then drift off to sleep . . .

. . . in their soft feather nests.